StoneSoup

Writing and art by kids, for kids

Editor's Note

I know March is winter still in most places, but I couldn't wait to celebrate spring and all it symbolizes—new life and new beginnings. As I write this from the end of 2020, I don't know what the winter will hold for all of us, but I feel sure that we will all be in need of many long, cleansing rains, big puddles to jump in, mud to squelch beneath our boots, tulip bulbs beginning to peek through the dirt, cherry blossoms, California poppies, rainbows, baby bunnies, fawns, songbird song, and everything else that comes with this wonderful season.

Most of this issue is about spring—in a literal sense (spring is coming!) and also a metaphorical one. "Spring"—in the form of growth and new life—is coming after an emotional "winter." Much of the writing in these pages tackles difficult experiences: divorce, fights with friends, moving, bullying, depression, and therapy. But what I love about these pieces is that the narrators are eventually able to see past their own feelings of isolation during these hard times, and to realize that these challenging experiences and difficult feelings are actually part of what connects us rather than keeps us apart.

Enjoy the almost-spring!

On the cover:
Sensation
(iPhone XS Max)
Aiyla Syed, 13
Asbury, NJ

Editor in Chief
Emma Wood

Director
William Rubel

Managing Editor
Jane Levi

Blog & Special Projects
Sarah Ainsworth

Design
Joe Ewart

Stone Soup (ISSN 0094 579X) is published eleven times per year—monthly, with a combined July/August summer issue. Copyright © 2021 by the Children's Art Foundation–Stone Soup Inc., a 501(c)(3) nonprofit organization located in Santa Cruz, California. All rights reserved.

Thirty-five percent of our subscription price is tax-deductible. Make a donation at Stonesoup.com/donate, and support us by choosing Children's Art Foundation as your Amazon Smile charity.

POSTMASTER: Send address changes to Stone Soup, 126 Otis Street, Santa Cruz, CA 95060. Periodicals postage paid at Santa Cruz, California, and additional offices.

Stone Soup is available in different formats to persons who have trouble seeing or reading the print or online editions. To request the braille edition from the National Library of Congress, call +1 800-424-8567. To request access to the audio edition via the National Federation of the Blind's NFB-NEWSLINE®, call +1 866-504-7300, or visit Nfbnewsline.org.

Submit your stories, poems, art, and letters to the editor via Stonesoup.submittable.com/submit. Subscribe to the print and digital editions at Stonesoup.com. Email questions about your subscription to Subscriptions@stonesoup.com. All other queries via email to Stonesoup@stonesoup.com.

Check us out on social media:

StoneSoup
Contents

Fly High in the Sky
(Watercolor)
Sloka Ganne, 11
Overland Park, KS

The Flowers That Live Forever

Olivia Judertt is determined to bring color to her gloomy, gray town

By Iris Chen, 10
Rye Brook, NY

A young girl walked through the gloomy roads of Brickville. As she walked, some rain began to fall.

Huh, the girl, whose name was Olivia Judertt, thought. *What perfect rain for flowers.*

Olivia loved her town, but it had no real color. She also didn't like the fact that the town had no flowers.

Olivia hated gloomy and gray things. She was very fond of flowers and color. Olivia loved coloring more than sketching, and she would rather get a colorful paint set than a phone as a gift. Her room was painted rainbow, and the first time you set eyes on it, you had to shield your eyes: the colors clashed together so much and it was too bright.

So when she noticed that the town was missing color and flowers, her two favorite things, she decided to change that.

One day she hopped into the kitchen with a new idea forming in her mind. "Mom, Dad!" she exclaimed. "I would like to plant some flowers in our backyard!"

Mrs. and Mr. Judertt laughed uneasily. "Oh, silly girl," they said. "The soil in our backyard isn't nice enough for some pretty flowers. Besides, the weather here is very foggy, and flowers need plenty of sun."

Stubborn Olivia refused to give up. She emptied her piggy bank and walked to the closest flower shop.

Olivia looked around the flower shop. Lots of colorless, grown flowers covered one side while seeds were stacked on top of each other on the other. She walked around, trying to pick out the just-right flowers. All the flowers there were expensive and not very colorful.

"This is hopeless," Olivia grumbled after half an hour of searching for the perfect seeds.

Then something caught her eye. On the top shelf at the back of the store, sitting proudly right behind two really ugly flowers, was the most beautiful and colorful flower Olivia had ever seen.

Olivia scrambled around for a stool to stand up on. She found one, climbed onto it, reached high, and brought down the flower.

"Oh, it's just a package," she said to herself. The name on the package really drew her interest, though. It read, "THE FLOWERS THAT LIVE FOREVER."

"That will be perfect!" she exclaimed as she took it off the shelf and brought it to the counter for checkout.

Olivia brought the flower package to the checkout center. She waited in line patiently with her heart thumping excitedly in her chest.

When it was her turn, she put the package in front of the clerk. The clerk looked at her strangely.

"Where'd ya get this package?" he asked. "We don't have no flowers that live forever. This package right here must be a fake. And where are your parents, kid?"

"My parents are at home," Olivia answered truthfully. "And I insist on having these seeds. I want them no matter what."

The clerk sighed, shaking his head. His red, fluffy beard swayed as his head shook. "Kids these days," he muttered.

Olivia left the flower shop feeling both happy and excited. She had finally bought flowers! This was her big day!

But she also felt that something fishy was going on with these flowers. The clerk had said that he'd never seen flowers like those before. He didn't recognize the flowers either.

Whatever, Olivia thought. *He probably just doesn't know the flowers in the store well enough.*

She raced over to her backyard and planted the flowers, following the instructions on the package.

When she'd finished planting, she ran back into the house to get her flower pillow. The pillow used to be gray; now it was rainbow. Olivia had taken out her homemade colorful permanent markers and colored every inch of the pillow to make it as colorful as possible. She had named the pillow Colory.

As she started going back outside, she felt a hand on her shoulder. She turned around. It was her mother.

"Olivia, honey," Mrs. Judertt said kindly, "where are you going in such a hurry with Colory?"

"I'm going to show Colory the flowers I planted!" Olivia said cheerfully.

Mrs. Judertt's jaw dropped and Mr. Judertt dropped his mug on the floor. As soon as the mug touched the ground, it shattered into a million pieces.

"You did what?" Mr. Judertt asked sharply.

"I planted flowers!" Olivia said happily.

"Lead me to them right away!" he ordered.

As he passed Mrs. Judertt, he whispered: "Get me a small knife."

Mrs. Judertt nodded quickly and went into the kitchen.

Olivia led her father to where she had planted the flower seeds. In this short amount of time, the flowers had already grown an inch.

"These flowers grow pretty quickly," Mr. Judertt said, trying to sound cheerful.

"I know," Olivia said, nodding and smiling thoughtfully.

Mrs. Judertt arrived with something clutched in her hand. She went straight to Mr. Judertt.

"Mommy," Olivia said curiously, "what's that in your hand?"

"Nothing you need to worry about, sweetie," Mrs. Judertt said sweetly.

She slipped the knife into Mr. Judertt's hand when Olivia wasn't looking. Mr. Judertt held the knife at the ready.

Olivia turned around just in time.

"No!" she screamed, flinging herself toward her father, "No! Please! What are you doing?"

"Get out of the way!" her father roared, "I don't want you to get hurt!"

"Don't. Mess. With. Me. And. My. FLOWERS!" Olivia said through gritted teeth, pulling on her father's arm to stop him.

"We can't get caught with colorful things!" Mr. Judertt shouted. "We must still keep colorless so no one will think we're crazy and insulting! The town is still grieving from the hurricane, and we must grieve with it!"

Suddenly Olivia stopped pulling. Mr. Judertt knew he had just spilled the beans. He dropped the knife and clapped a hand over his mouth. Mrs. Judertt stared at the ground.

"A hurricane?" Olivia said slowly. "Grieving? How do I not know about this?"

"You were not yet born," Mrs. Judertt said softly.

"I mean, why didn't anyone tell me *after* I was born?" Olivia asked.

"We wanted you to have a happy, carefree life with no hurricane and no grieving," Mr. Judertt sighed. "We

should've told you. But even if we had told you, you were too little to understand."

Olivia stared at her parents for a long time. Then her face lit up.

"That's perfect!" she cried, dancing around. "I'll make everyone happy by planting flowers in their backyards!"

"Don't you dare, Olivia!" Mrs. Judertt yelled as she chased after her daughter. Of course, she was too slow.

Olivia took the rest of the seeds and raced around Brickville, planting flowers here and there. As she ran around planting all the flowers, people peeked through their drawn curtains and gasped. They knew that the mayor was going to talk to them about disrespecting the ones who had died during the hurricane.

The flowers grew fast. Soon, colorful flowers were all over town. The mayor of Brickville, Mayor Incolore, was angry that a little girl was planting flowers all over a grieving town.

"This Olivia Judertt must be stopped!" he declared over the radio one morning.

When Olivia heard the news, all she did was plant more flowers. She didn't care what other people thought.

Someday, she told herself. *Someday they will understand.*

For his family's safety, Mr. Judertt found another house and they moved out of town. The Judertt family's old house remained empty. No one wanted to move into a colorless town with a mayor screaming for some innocent little girl to be stopped.

One day, Mayor Incolore retired. He was very old now, and he was tired of looking around for Olivia Judertt. The next mayor was Mayor Apono. This mayor didn't care about the flowers. Instead, he focused on more important things, like raising money for the poor.

"Before, we were all looking backward and to the past," he said, "But the thing we should have been doing and will do is look forward to the future and make the world a better place. The past is past; there's no way to change it. The hurricane must always be in our history, but that doesn't mean we should be grieving all the time. Brighten up and think about what the future holds for us!"

Soon, people from other towns heard about this amazing place with beautiful, colorful flowers that never seemed to die. They heard about this nice little girl who had planted them, and how the goodness and cheerfulness in her heart never seemed to end. Rumor has it that it was the kindness of the little girl that made the flowers so colorful and long-living. Tourists came from all over the world, and the money that the flowers made for Brickville cured all of the town's troubles.

People started liking the flowers. In fact, the people took exceptionally good care of the colorful flowers in their backyards! The people watered them and let them have plenty of sunlight. They also picked out any weeds growing anywhere near their precious flowers.

Mayor Apono was named best mayor of the decade, and Brickville had its happily ever after. Sure, sometimes there were small problems here and there, but all in all, Brickville was a lightened, colorful town. Olivia's dream had come true. She had helped the people in need, and now the town was colorful. Although Olivia wasn't there to see it, all her hard work paid off.

Now people were fighting over Olivia's old house. Everyone wanted to live in the house of the girl who had changed the town.

Brickville and its amazing flowers are still there today.

Always remember: a good heart can change the world.

ARTIST PORTFOLIO

Five Photographs

By Sage Millen, 12
Vancouver, Canada
(Canon PowerShot SX600)

MARCH 2021

9

Artist's statement

I got into dance photography about three years ago. Looking back on that first photo shoot with dancer Lizzie Garraway, 13, who is featured as the solo dancer in all of these photographs, we both cringe. We have both improved so much that all we can see in those early photographs are our errors. We're still improving—as somebody once said (I forget who), "Dancers strive for perfection. Once you're perfect, why bother dancing?" The same goes for photography. I submitted this portfolio only a month or two ago, and I can already see areas for improvement—Lizzie didn't wing her foot, or the photo isn't quite straight, among other things. That said, I'm excited to share these images with you, and I hope you enjoy them.

The hardest photo to take was "*Heart but Apart*," because of two elements: first, there are two dancers, and second, they are both jumping. It's difficult for two dancers to be perfectly coordinated. On the rare occasion that it did happen, usually at least one of them wasn't satisfied with their jump. This photo must have taken at least twenty jumps! Also, I post-edited it a bit—it was taken in low light and my camera isn't amazing, so I just brightened the colors a little and added some vignette.

The easiest photo to take was probably "*Love*." I saw this mural and thought it would be a great location for dance photography. The more I take photos, the more I notice locations and think, "Hey, this would be a great background!" Even if you think there are no good locations for photography near you, trust me, there are. Anyway, it took us a few tries to get the pose right but once we had that down, it took only seconds to get a shot we both liked.

Things you want to keep in mind for dance photography include: location, model, pose, wardrobe, lighting, and angles. Usually, the dancer should be wearing bright, colorful and tight-fitting clothes, unless you're going for a specific theme. A flowy dress could work as long as you consider how that will affect the dancer's lines and mobility.

If you've never tried dance photography—give it a chance! You might enjoy it. Also, most people are flattered if you want to take photos of them—I was nervous asking Lizzie and her sister Ana, 15, (who is featured in "*Heart but Apart*") for the first time even though we're good friends. Luckily, they agreed, and we've had so much fun ever since—even when the photos didn't turn out!

Sunset Silhouette

Stag on the Skyline

Firebird

Love …

Heart but Apart

Believing

Waiting to hear if she and her dance teammates won nationals, Lily reflects on the ups and downs they met along the way

By Lily Shi, 11
Saratoga, CA

I walked onstage slowly, following the dancer in front of me. I was sweating up my costume, partly because of the intense heat coming from the blazing stage lights overhead and partly because of the anxious anticipation. I peered into the audience, trying to find my grandma. My eyes traveled over hundreds of people, tall and short, young and old, but from the stage, they all looked the same. All I could see in front of me were rows and rows of seats, not a single one empty.

The stage itself was humongous. Colorful lights hung from a beam on the ceiling, illuminating the large wooden platform. Velvety violet curtains—three on each side—hung indifferently from the rafters backstage. On the large screen, fixed on the back wall of the stage, the Kids Artistic Revue (KAR) logo was projected in an enormous purple font. After a long wait, the audience murmured like the gallery at a trial as two men wearing black suits stepped onstage carrying a towering trophy. At first, the trophy looked shiny black, but as the men set it in the center of the stage and it caught the light, rainbow hues flashed magically across its long metal rods, thrilling me.

I gulped nervously as a woman with long, curly red hair came striding up to the stage holding a giant piece of paper. Quickly, the cavernous auditorium became eerily quiet. Squinting, I managed to see the number 200 written on an oversized check; it was the $200 prize to be awarded to the winning dance team— the National Grand Champion.

Out of nowhere, a feeling of dread shot through my body, and I shivered despite the invisible glow of heat radiating from above. My team had won first place in the first round, and we had survived the secondary round to make it into Showcase, the finals, our chance to win the ultimate prize. Just a few of the original fifty squads had to be bested, and I kept thinking that it would be a shame to have gone so far just to lose in the showcase round. Of course, the other teams were probably thinking this way too. I glanced around the stage, where the eight other teams had formed a half circle.

What were the chances that we would win?

> "I yearned to feel the thrill of dancing on stage for a large audience, but my family was too poor to afford dance lessons, and my parents couldn't even afford to buy me dance shoes. Eventually, I gave up on my dream".

I thought back to the regional competition three months earlier when our team had received a low score. On stage, we had been wobbly and messy, and everyone had returned home embarrassed and sad. Afterward, there was even talk about forfeiting our spot in nationals because of our poor performance in the regionals. When I'd heard some of the rumors flying around, I was upset. To me, there was no doubt: we absolutely had to go to nationals! After how hard we had worked, and how long, we couldn't, after one bad performance, just give up. Luckily for me, our tough-as-iron instructor, Ms. Lu, agreed. Instead of letting us give up, she demanded that we work harder than ever and pushed us to our limits. Slowly, our form improved, and a twinkling of hope began to reappear. Day after day, we rehearsed for hours, and now, three months later, we were at nationals. As far as I was concerned, we had to win to prove those disbelievers wrong.

As we stood there waiting, the passing seconds felt like hours. I found myself nervously fingering a long tear in my skirt, one that had been cleverly patched up with a long white thread that had rendered it practically invisible. And, oddly, touching the thread triggered a memory.

My mind drifted back to the day after our defeat at regionals, when my beloved grandma was sitting on the couch in our living room, sewing the rips in my costume, rips that had occurred on the rough competition stage. "You can do it, Li-li," she said to me, sensing my lack of self-confidence.

I stopped whatever I was doing, walked over, and sat next to her. Her warm, gentle voice and soft smile, along with her soft curls, hid an inner toughness.

"Never give up," she said to me in perfect Mandarin. "When I was a young girl like you, I lived in a small town in China called Shantou. My dream was to be a professional dancer. I would secretly watch dance performances on television and search magazines for pictures of elegant dancers and paste them on my bedroom wall. I would lock myself in my room and dance to some music, glancing longingly at those pictures. I yearned to feel the thrill of dancing on stage for a large audience, but my family was too poor to afford dance lessons, and my parents couldn't even afford to buy me dance shoes. Eventually, I gave up on my dream. You cannot, Li-li," she said to me, her eyes sparkling with a deep determination that I didn't have.

I nodded earnestly and gave her a tender smile. "Don't worry, Grandma," I reassured her. "We can do it." I held her delicate hand for a few more seconds and then left, a warm feeling in my chest and a new motivation burning in my heart.

Our team, consisting of sixteen

nine-year-old girls, had spent many months learning a dance called "Everybody Do the Cancan." It was a cabaret-style jazz dance, and the highlight was a very difficult sequence that came in the middle of the performance. At a precise time, all sixteen of us would form a straight, horizontal line and, while kicking our legs high and together as one, complete a 360-degree turn. It had to be done with the utmost precision in order to really wow the audience, and we knew it would make or break our score. I remembered how, during rehearsals, Ms. Lu had told me my kicks were too slow, my toes not pointed, and my knees not straight enough. We spent countless hours trying to perfect that single move, but for the longest time, I couldn't get it right. The feeling of letting down my teammates and having them repeat the same movements again and again because of my mistakes was seared into my memory.

One day, Grandma had come to rehearsal, like she often did, to pick me up, and that day, she came extra early in order to peer through the window and watch me practice. As a result, she had witnessed Ms. Lu lecturing me about my form. When practice was over, she noticed that I was dejected and sad, my shoulders drooping, and as I told her what Ms. Lu had said about my knees, a look of indignation crossed her face. "I don't know what you're talking about, Li-li," she said. "You were the best one there. I think Ms. Lu was talking about someone else." I almost laughed. Grandma always knew how to make me feel better.

My mind then drifted to the spare room in our house and the many hours spent on the cold hardwood floor practicing that movement, my knees dark bluish purple from falling, until I finally conquered this most difficult maneuver. It had turned out to be worth it, for much like a jazz guitarist must feel after conquering an especially difficult solo, the thrill that ran through my body as I executed the movement perfectly during the showcase was indescribably wonderful.

Just then, I was shocked into the present as one of the men loudly cleared his throat while holding up a microphone. My eyes flickered across the audience as I searched vainly for Grandma. "And the national grand champion for Primary Large Group is . . ."

The audience seemed to plummet into a black hole of silence. I could feel myself holding my breath. Next to me, my teammate Ashley whispered, "I can't listen!" and covered her ears. I tried to smile but was frozen still with excited fear.

We had to win. We had to! *Please . . .*

All of those long hours at practices, all of those bruised knees and sore ankles and muscles . . .

I watched as the man's mouth began to open. In slow motion, as if he were mute, he seemed to struggle to open his mouth . . .

Finally, he yelled, "'Everybody Do the Cancan'!!!"

Yep. I thought. I knew it. *We didn't win.*

Then my brain processed the true meaning of what he had just said.

My eyebrows shot to the stars, my

My eyebrows shot to the stars, my eyes widened to the size of saucers, and my jaw dropped to the ground.

eyes widened to the size of saucers, and my jaw dropped to the ground. In the corner of my consciousness, I heard someone screaming—a scream loud enough to shatter glass. Then I realized it was me. My teammates were screaming too, but it felt like my scream—so full of shock, relief, and elation—had blanketed the room.

Shrieking, all sixteen of us dashed to the trophy and the $200 check, claiming both as ours in the biggest and best group hug of all time. And while the other teams trudged off the stage, my teammates and I admired the trophy, which was twice our height. Smiles beamed from ear to ear as hundreds of individual and group photos were taken next to the massive award. Instinctively, I searched the crowd once again for my grandma, and this time I spotted her sitting in the second row, a huge smile and glistening eyes radiating from her face. As I watched her, her eyes seemed to say, "You did it."

I don't remember every single little detail about what happened next since the elation had blurred my thinking, but I do remember a journalist walking up to us and asking us how we felt. Someone shouted, "We feel good!" That was followed by some laughter and more voices calling, "Yeah, we feel really good!"

The trophy looked spectacular in our dance studio—shiny, tall, and colorful. Every time I looked at it, I would feel a surge of pride as I remembered what it took to win that coveted prize.

Several weeks later, when we threw a party in honor of our team's achievement, the winning of the National Grand Championship, the entire team gathered in the studio; we ate cake while watching videos of our performances that weekend. We also watched the fateful moment when the judge had announced the winner many times. It felt great, but by that time the glow had already begun to fade slightly. For by then we were all thinking, "*Tomorrow we'll be back in the studio, in our leotards and high buns, ready to bruise our knees and test our ankles in our quest to win next year's competition.*"

But for one last moment, after everyone else had left, I waited for the light to catch the metal rods on the trophy just right and send rainbow hues flying in all directions. And when it did, I felt the thrill one last time, this time for my precious grandma.

Good Time
(Procreate)
Emi Le, 13
Millbrae, CA

Moving to a Familiar Place

Tallulah knows that moving to a bigger home is a good thing— but it's still hard to say goodbye

By Georgia Melnick, 12
Highland Park, NJ

My sister and I lived in a small yellow house with a bright-blue door. The roof was white and so was the porch. The stairs were a bland tan, but I actually liked them a lot because they were familiar.

Delilah (she's my sister) and I shared a room. We only had enough space for a bunk bed and a dresser. I was on the top bunk and she was on the bottom. We each had sheets that were blue. Our bed was in the corner of the room, the corner closest to the big window. By "big" I mean "small," but it was the biggest window we had ever seen. We had pictures of each other on the pretty purple walls. We loved our room.

Our parents' room was next to ours. Our parents had a bed and two dressers and two small mirrors. A bigger mirror was hung on the door. Though it was still slightly bigger than our room, it was still small.

We had old-people neighbors, and none of us had a lot of money. The streets were mostly dirty, though once a year the street sweepers came in and did the top part of the street,

leaving most of the street unkempt.

Only a week ago, we had found out that we were moving. My parents were really excited, but not me. Delilah was hopeful, but not me. This is what my mother said: "Tallulah? Haven't you always wanted to live in a bigger house and go to a better school? This will be your chance!"

I suppose I had, but I didn't want to leave my street. So I just shook my head up and down.

"You will have a bigger room and more space for things you like!" my father answered.

"But Dad, I don't want to move! Aren't we happy here?"

"Tallulah, your mother and I are bigger than you and Delilah. We need more room."

"Hey, I want to go outside," Delilah interrupted.

"Go outside with your sister, Tallulah."

I grabbed her and darted out of the house. By the way, I am ten and Delilah is five. Outside, we played in the nice green grass. Imagine the prettiest blue dress you've ever seen; that's what the sky looked like. I remember Delilah doing cartwheels across the grass. She begged me to play with her, so I did. After a while, my friend walked by and stayed with me.

"I heard you were moving."

"Yeah."

"Where are you going?"

"A town away."

"Oh." Delilah stopped doing cartwheels and sat down right in my friend's lap.

"Hi, Gracie," she said.

"Hi, Delilah! I'm gonna miss you and Tallulah a lot."

"I know. I will miss you and Devon. Where is she?"

"Oh, she's at my house. I can call her over."

Devon was Gracie's little sister; she was also five. Gracie ran down the street to get Devon; they only lived three houses down. Gracie eventually returned with Devon in her arms. No other kids lived on the street, so we were lucky that Gracie was my age and Devon was Delilah's. Delilah played dolls with Devon, and Gracie and I played hopscotch. After a while, we all played tag, which was kind of hard since Delilah and Devon were so young.

"Oh no, you got me!" I yelled when Devon tapped my arm.

"Tallulah's it!" Gracie called, running with my sister's hand in hers.

Once our legs got wobbly and our breath was scarce, we went inside and my mom made us dinner.

Everything was pretty normal the rest of the week—just packing and such. But when the week was over our parents threw a big party, and our parents' friends came over for dinner and so did mine and Delilah's. Gracie and Devon were the first people there. Next came my friend Lena and her baby brother, Alan.

"Hi, Tallulah," she said, hugging me.

"Hello, Tallulah! Hello, Delilah! We were very sad to hear that you were leaving," Lena's mom said, coming into our house. For some reason, when Delilah's in the room, adults do that thing where they are very loud and they over-articulate.

Lena, Gracie, and I left together and went into the small backyard. Since our house was pretty small, the party leaked over into the backyard, front porch, and front yard. I thought it was a lot of fuss since we were only moving a town away, but I think our parents wanted us to leave on a happy note.

I don't remember where Delilah went once all of her friends showed up, but my friends and I stayed in the backyard and played card games, and eventually we went inside and played Mario video games that my friends Luke and Livie (they are twins) brought.

"And Tallulah Ross takes the lead!"

"Come on, girls! Time to get up!" my dad is calling from downstairs. "We have got a lot of things to start moving!"

"Dad," I ask, "how will we sleep there tonight?"

"We have a very special surprise."

"Surprise?" Delilah asks, suddenly jumping up.

"Your mother and I purchased

The reason we are moving is that our dad got a new job and he gets paid much more money. It's a good thing, I guess.

sleeping bags!"

"You have got to be kidding me." I slump back down into my bed.

"Come on, Tallulah. It will be fun to sleep on the floor of our new house." Our dad shakes the bed, which makes me even more mad. I hop out of bed and hold my sister's hand. I follow the smell of pancakes downstairs.

"That smells so yummy!"

"Thank you, Delilah!" my mom says as she picks my sister up.

As soon as we are done, she tells us to go and get dressed.

"Wear something comfortable!" she yells behind us.

"Tallulah, let's wear matching."

"Sure." I smile. We put on black sweatpants and plain purple shirts and grey sweaters. I put Delilah's hair in two French braids, which always makes her look adorable. Then I do the same to myself. We both have dirty-blonde hair and green eyes. We both put on sneakers and then go back downstairs with backpacks full of stuff. Then we get in the car. Before I step in, I step back and look toward the grass, then at the little yellow house. The old familiar house. Finally, I step into the car.

"Bye, Big Bird!" my sister and I call out.

"See ya, old friend!" my parents say. "We'll be back soon to get more stuff, girls. Don't worry."

I smile, but tears are forming in my eyes as I watch.

The reason we are moving is that our dad got a new job and he gets paid much more money. It's a good

thing, I guess.

_____

When we get to our new house, I am amazed.

"We must be rich!" I say, nudging my dad.

"I knew you would like it, Tallulah!"

"Delilah!" I grab her hand and we race into the house. "Whoah! Our room is so much bigger!"

"Our bed should go here." She points to the corner near the window.

"Perfect," I reply. "We should put the dresser here." I point to the other side of the room. Dad says the movers won't be here for another week.

For dinner we have pizza, and since we don't have the TV yet, we watch Delilah sing.

"It's raining," I say, and Delilah breaks out into the song "It's Raining, It's Pouring."

"Perfect night for a sleepover!" Dad yells with a clap. He grabs the blankets and sleeping bags, and we all cuddle up together the best we can.

"Night night!" Delilah says.

"Goodnight!" we all answer.

_____

About a week later, all the stuff is moved in. I like it here a lot, and so do my sister and our parents. We are going to start school in another week. I'm kind of excited because it's one of the top schools in the state, but I'm going to have to make new friends. I already met one girl on the street. Her name is Maze. She seems nice.

That afternoon, I'm sitting outside

on the porch like I used to at my old house. Gracie and Devon aren't just gonna walk past, though. I miss them. I miss my friends. I don't want to be here alone anymore.

"Tallulah! Delilah! Come to the kitchen," we hear.

"Yes, Daddy?"

"Girls, we have a special surprise! Guess who's living in the Big Bird?" he said, wrapping his arms around me. I guess he could see my glossy eyes.

"Who?" I asked.

"Your Aunt Millie and Diamond!" I suddenly felt ten times better. She is my mom's sister; she has one kid (Diamond).

"Really?"

"Yep! And we get to visit her!"

Thank you, Aunt Millie! I think. I am so happy; I think we all are.

Delilah and I decide to take a walk to the ice cream shop down the street. The move was treacherous, but the best part about it was that there is a perfect ice cream shop nearby called Bella's Creamery. Bella is the owner's daughter. She's in high school, and she works there during the summer. I like her; she always has a smile, and she remembers us. Every time we go over there, she smiles and says, "Tallulah and Delilah! The H sisters!" She says this because we both have an H at the end of our names.

Soon it is bedtime. I am tired, unlike most nights. The wind is whistling outside; it had been a perfect night.

"Thanks, Daddy," I whisper.

"I love you, girls," he replies softly with a smile.

Suddenly, this new home feels a whole lot more familiar.

Baseball Memories
(Colored pencil)
Lauren Yu, 13
Cresskill, NJ

A Windy Spring Day

Two next-door-neighbors-turned-best-friends share a quiet afternoon together

By Jack Meyer, 13
Brooklyn, NY

I am poking my head through a hole in my fence, a fence made of oak that gives me splinters when I touch it. It creaks and squeaks when it is pushed. The raspberry bushes and plum trees are blown against it by the wind.

The vines of the raspberry bushes climb up the old fence, blooming with new flowers—white and pink berries too, the kind that make me cringe when they hit my tongue. The hole is small. I can barely fit through it now—not easily as I used to.

It's quiet-yet-loud with the deafening sound of leaves wrestling each other in the wind. I break the roaring silence. I yell, "Kyle!" My voice inflects the same way one does when asking a question.

There is a vociferous pause as the wind picks up and lets out a quiet scream. The inconsistent and forceful sound of a screen door sliding off its track breaks the blaring stillness. The mesh of the screen hits the wood of the house as the wind forces it back. The door slides in, surges a little bit, pauses, then a little bit more.

It's a windy, hot spring day in California. The smell of honeysuckle and chlorine from the neighbor's pool can be smelled from houses away. A dog barks from a few houses down. Rick's motorcycle pulls into his driveway. A squirrel dashes across our lawn and up the stump of the oak tree.

Fifteen seconds go by, but it feels like thirty. A high-pitched voice calls back: "Yeah?"

The voice belongs to a boy named Kyle. He and I have known each other for years. We go to the same school, White Oaks Elementary. He was four when I met him. I was three. He didn't have many friends. I didn't either.

We are next-door neighbors and have been for five years. He and I are very different. He is shy and quiet with people he doesn't know. He hates math; he really hates it. He tried to pull the "my cat ate my math homework" excuse a few weeks ago. Kyle thought it would work. He even took a photo of his cat sitting down next to the crumpled up homework using his iPod Touch. His parents weren't very happy. I thought that was hilarious.

Kyle sees his parents a lot and has never spent more than a few days away from them. My parents travel a lot. I spend a few nights a year at

Kyle's. It isn't as much of a problem having school in the morning as we have to walk just two blocks to get there. At our sleepovers we play Nerf guns and ride our bikes up and down the same hill till the sun sets. I always wanted my own Nerf guns, but my mom wouldn't let me have any.

Kyle is a Boy Scout and a baseball player. I played T-ball once. I quit shortly after.

We have gone to the same marine biology camp every summer since we met; we always win the knot-tying competition.

The wind throws a leaf into my face. It is sharp and dry, but it doesn't scratch my skin.

The hole in the fence leads straight into his backyard. His cat, Mercedes, seems to live at the top of that fence. Her big green eyes are the first thing I notice when I see her. She is small and timid. Her shoulders point out when she crouches, and her ribs poke out when she stands. She doesn't like people that much. She doesn't like anything that much. She likes that fence, though.

I hear footsteps on wet grass and peer through the hole. I squeeze through the hole shoulder-first, and Kyle greets me with a bowl of mint chocolate chip ice cream and a wide, toothless smile. His dad, Rick, is a strong believer in mint chip. After dinner, he always pulls out a quart of the stuff and drops it on the dinner table dramatically.

Kyle just got back from Mexico, his first trip outside of the country. We talk about it as we eat our mint chocolate chip ice cream on the big leather couch in the living room,

knowing his mom would be furious if she saw us. She loves that couch.

The green scoops start melting. Kyle loves ice cream soup; I don't. I pick up my pace, talk less and listen more as we stop talking about his trip to Mexico and move on to our thoughts on the elusive purple shore crab.

When we are done with our mid-afternoon dessert, we turn on the Wii. We like to play *Super Mario Brothers*. I'm always Mario. He's always Luigi. He always goes for the highest points and most stars. I go for the least time and most lives. Kyle is much better at *Super Mario Brothers* than I am—not like that's saying much. We've been stuck fighting in Bowser's castle on the same level for a few months now. Thirty minutes pass. Mario falls into the lava and Luigi is the only one left. After much smashing of buttons, Luigi falls into the lava, and we hear the same low-pitched Bowser laugh for the hundredth time.

The big grandfather clock in his living room goes off. It is six o'clock. I can hear my mom calling my name from my backyard.

Spring

By Andy Li, 7
Hong Kong, China

Spring is green
People roam about
Roars fill the jungle air
Iguanas sleep in the trees
New flowers are blooming
Great

Brewing Trouble

A tense moment sparks a meditation on friendship

By Oliver Cho, 12
Hillsborough, CA

Friends. Friends whose shouts are the reverberating crash of ocean waves on a rocky cliff, slowly sanding down its rough edges in the way that we shape each other. Like the slow ascension of water as it marches up the steady inclination of a beach. Those are my friends.

I stand still, watching a distant world whiz by me. The world moves around me without noticing my presence. My head spins. I hear a shout echo around me, but I am unable to discern its location.

Suddenly, my world comes into view. A wooden patio bench with a glossy metal frame stained from the numerous foods spilled on it. An opaque wall with the silhouettes of people on the other side like a Halloween jack-o'-lantern. I share a brief smile with my distorted reflection, but soon I feel the tension in the area rising like the unavoidable sparks of a future wildfire, and my instincts kick in.

In the moments that my back was turned, something terrible has taken place. I look back on what happened with the discerning eyes of an eagle. A broken plate, potatoes on the floor, two angry kids, and one authoritative figure. A single result. A single result that had to end this way—shattered work, waste, anger, and authority. Thoughts about a reasonable explanation fill my head like an ocean about to overflow, but one stands out like a red balloon in a monochrome movie. I hold onto that idea like a mountain climber grasping onto the side of a mountain with a single hand, waiting for the time when the howling winds will die down.

A thorough search for an explanation commences until one is found. The kids, deflated like two flat tires, regretfully describe the cause with an apology brewing in their mind. I stand there, my original idea reinforced with the steel of command. We talk for an hour. A whole hour, until we settle the issue and prepare to leave it in the waiting hands of the past.

For a brief moment, we all share a look, and a realization crosses our minds the way sunlight gracefully prances across the lush fields of vegetation. We share a smile. My friends, even though they may cause trouble, will always figure things out.

Sunny Beach
(Procreate)
Emi Le, 13
Millbrae, CA

Sand and Sea

When her parents tell her they're getting a divorce, Kate runs away

By Raya Ilieva, 10
Belmont, CA

Smooth waves of water crested up out of the foamy blue sea and crashed down on the empty beach, rushing out along a darkened strip of sand, and then were sucked back into the depths of the blue ocean. Kate paced the rough sand, gritty crystals coating her bare feet and tickling her ankles. A heavy fog hung over the beach, covering the sky and the air in a thick gray mass that did nothing to help lighten Kate's mood.

Her usually warm light-gray eyes were stormy, dark, and wild and focused on the never-ending expanse of sand and water before her, dotted by washed-up shells and pieces of driftwood. Her strides were purposeful and determined, carrying her across the beach in a direction that seemed to go on forever. Kate was fine with that. She did not want to go back to her house, now just a small blue dot on top of the hill. Kate walked faster.

While normally Kate would stop to brush the sand off of her feet before continuing on, such a thought never even entered her mind now. She was set only on walking as far away from her house as possible. She tried not to think about the things she loved about it: the creaky stair; the fading blue paint that she herself had picked out; the kitchen table with many scratches from her cat, Rocket, who refused to use his beautiful scratching post and instead ruined their furniture; her bedroom with the glow-in-the-dark star stickers and pale blue bedspread, among some things. The reason Kate did not want to think about her house was because she was leaving. Forever, at least in her mind.

Her parents were getting a divorce. They had sat her down last night at the kitchen table and announced it. Kate had sat there gaping for a moment. Then when it had sunk in, she had jumped up from the kitchen table, not minding the chair that had crashed to the ground, and raced upstairs, slamming the door to her bedroom.

She had heard her parents fighting. But it was never about anything serious. They weren't even fights— more like arguments, whispered conversations late at night that Kate could hear. She had thought nothing of it. Until the Announcement.

To make matters worse, her parents had used formal names. They

All she could think about was her warm, warm bed with Rocket sitting on top of it on his usual place on her pillow.

had called each other "Marina" and "Aleksander" instead of Mom and Dad, and—worst of all—"Katarina" for Kate. She had certain opinions of her own about her name.

When they had called her "Katarina," she had just about exploded. That was when she had slammed her door. She had slept fitfully that night and in the morning decided to run away and find a better life. So here she was on the beach.

Wind sailed across the beach, twisting and turning and blowing Kate's long, dark braid out behind her. Locks got dislodged and tangled together, pulling on Kate's scalp. She tucked her braid into the collar of her shirt. Not thinking, she had not brought a jacket. The cold turned Kate's cheeks rosy. She hid her face by her neck.

Wind howled in Kate's ears. Her bare feet turned cold. The thoughts inside her brain roiled around like a thunderstorm. But still she walked.

When at last she found a small cave in the side of the rocky cliffs bordering the beach, Kate was almost faint from exhaustion and cold. Searching for somewhere to sit, she eventually curled up in the corner by a pile of driftwood. Something slimy rubbed against her leg. Kate stifled a scream. But it was only a piece of kelp by her feet. She breathed a sigh of relief.

Her throat felt dry and hoarse. In her haste to leave, she had not thought to bring any food or water. Or, for that matter, anything. Kate tried her best

not to swallow or speak. Suddenly, she missed her cat, Rocket.

She could imagine his soft, furry body nestling up in her arms. She would stroke his white fur, especially the brown patch near his throat. He would purr and she would feel satisfied and happy. Kate choked back a sob and rubbed her eyes fiercely to dry the tears that had collected there. She put her head on her knees.

All she could think about was her warm, warm bed with Rocket sitting on top of it on his usual place on her pillow. She could imagine the star stickers on her ceiling glowing cheerfully and the faded, warm wood of her bookshelf covered in different colorful spines.

Now Kate couldn't hold back the sobs. They racked her body as she buried her face in her hands and cried until she could cry no more. Looking out at the beach, she finally came to her senses. There was no way she could survive out here with no food or water or clothes; she knew that there were no neighbors she could go turn to for help, and after all, she was only twelve. Sighing, she stared at the beach. The rhythm of the waves crashing on the beach and then receding calmed her. She sat as if in a trance, mesmerized by the beach as she always was.

Finally, she worked up the will to go back. Standing up, she stretched out her long legs and began to walk. Soon she was running, her feet pounding the ground and sending up mini geysers of sand. Wind rushed at her and she welcomed it. Her feet touched the ground only long enough for them to send her up again.

Her house became more than a blue speck on the horizon. Coming into view, she could see the white shutters and fading wood. Her lungs were burning and there was a stitch in her side, but still she ran. Finally, she neared the wooden steps leading down to the beach.

Not caring about splinters in her raw, bare feet, she darted up the stairs and onto the prickly plants in the sand lining the walkway to her house. When her feet touched cool, gray concrete, she stopped to catch her breath.

When she felt more composed, she opened the door to her house. Her mother was sitting there, waiting with a cup of hot chocolate in her hands. Rocket was sprawled over Kate's chair. She picked him up and sat down, the cat in her lap.

Sipping from the hot mug, she felt its warmth go down her spine. An unexpected thought entered her mind: *This is what love feels like. And my parents still love me even if they don't love each other. Maybe that's okay.*

As if on cue, her father came in and sat on the other side of Kate, wrapping his arm around one shoulder while her mother got the other shoulder. They stayed like that for a while, a family, and Kate knew that her parents knew that she was okay about the divorce right now. She relished the moment, snuggled between her mother and her father with Rocket in her lap. A family, at least for the time being.

They don't understand

By Alyssa Wu, 13
Pleasanton, CA

No one believes I am depressed.
Depression becomes a privilege.
People are eager to make judgments and suggestions—
They never really know what I am going through.

Depression becomes a privilege.
To others I have a perfect life—
They never really know what I am going through.
I don't know how to end this feeling.

To others I have a perfect life.
No one hears my silent struggling.
I don't know where to end this feeling—
It's a part of who am I.

No one hears my silent struggling—
People think I am trying to find excuses.
It's a part of who am I.
No one believes I am depressed.

Mom's Kitchen

Mom is sick—
a sad thought but
there is one benefit:
I can finally occupy the kitchen,
the forbidden land of war
where you come out with scars, but always
a reward.

I wear my mother's green apron
like armor on the battlefield.
I treat ingredients with passion,
sprinkle the seasoning carefully,
make sure to clean up.

With a little bit of confidence,
a trace of nervousness and panic,
I push the pizza
into the oven,
hoping to surprise her.

Floating aroma,
a good heart,
and dedication—
all for my mom.

Buzzing Among Flowers
(Nikon Coolpix L830)
Hannah Parker, 13
South Burlington, VT

Spring Rain

The spring rain lightly
kisses the soil,
planting seeds

that become buds,
where hidden tender
petals lay,

a promise of bloom
that becomes
plum flowers
swaying in the wind with
silent beauty.

Thank You, Bernie

A mysterious girl joins Bernadette's group therapy sessions

By Sadie Primack, 13
Fayetteville, AR

"Bernadette."

As Miss Hunt says it, her voice seems far away. I'm sitting on one of the cold, grey chairs in the small, stuffy room they put the kids in. I've been told that my loose, grey sweatshirt with the hood up—and my baggy jeans—give me a scary, mysterious vibe. And that's the reason I wear them.

Miss Hunt's shouting jolts me back to the present. "Bernadette! I know you may not like going to therapy, but it can help you. So please participate!"

I feel the stares of the other people in the room. They're waiting to see what I will do next.

Guess I should give the people what they want. A little drama.

I sit up from my slouch and roll my eyes. "Fine. I'm feeling just swell. Really. I don't even know why I'm at therapy. My parents died ten years ago. I'm over it. Really."

Miss Hunt doesn't seem happy with my answer.

Determined to leave it at that, I look away. Four seats away from me sits a girl. She looks about my age—fourteen. She has shoulder-length straight, blonde hair with a thin blue streak starting at her left temple. She has big hazel eyes and freckles. She's wearing a Paddington-style navy blue coat, black tights, and chunky black combat boots. I don't know why I didn't notice her until now, though this is my first therapy session. It doesn't matter.

We are finally released. My uncle texts me, letting me know he's waiting outside. As I'm walking out the door, the Paddington-coat girl bumps into me, and I fall back a step. I catch a faceful of her hair.

I wish I had hair like that, I think, staring at my ugly, knotted ginger hair that my uncle won't let me dye because "it's so beautiful" and "it won't grow back the same."

I jolt back.

"I'm so sorry!" she says. "I didn't mean to. I just wanted to catch you before you left."

"Um, why?" I'm only partially effective at restraining my snarl.

"You, um, just seemed cool. I wanted to know your deal. I'm Sam." She blushes.

The girl stares at me. I stare back at her.

"Bernadette."

Colossal Clouds
(Canon PowerShot G9 X)
Anya Geist, 13
Worcester, MA

I don't care if Sam and I aren't friends. It might be better that way anyway.

Sam seems mysterious and cool, and potential friend material. Which means I have to stay as far away as possible from her.

———————————

The following week, I find myself back in that bleak therapy room, in that cold, uncomfortable chair, looking at that annoying Miss Hunt. She's not a bad person, but she doesn't get us. I'm in a black sweatshirt today, black leggings, and high-top white sneakers.

"So," Miss Hunt turns to a boy a few seats away from me. "What's going on, Charlie?"

The boy looks down at his feet. "Um, I guess I keep having these flashbacks and nightmares."

"What are they about, if you don't mind me asking?"

The boy shrinks further down. He looks at Miss Hunt but keeps his mouth shut.

I tune out the rest of the session until Miss Hunt questions Sam.

I shoot up from my slouching position.

"Nothing much. Just the usual," Sam replies. Miss Hunt and Sam share a look, obviously hiding something.

Great.

I know I shouldn't talk to Sam, but I want to know what's happening.

I walk up to Sam after the session. "What's your deal?" I ask.

"What do you mean?" she replies evenly.

"You know what I'm talking about. That look with Miss Hunt when she asked you a question. So, spill."

"Now, why should I tell you?" Sam smiles and heads out the door.

———————————

I'm sitting on my bedroom floor on top of a colorful rug my uncle picked out for me when I first moved into his house after my parents died. Sitting in front of me is the notebook Miss Hunt gave me a few days ago. It's silver with a rainbow hummingbird on the front. Do I have any intention of actually using it? Of course not. Journaling is for losers. But also, do I have emotions that I would like to express? Yes.

You know what? Screw it. I'll write in this stupid notebook.

I move across my room to grab a pen, my favorite one. It's blue and cheap, and I got it when I was going into sixth grade. It somehow survived that long. I like it because it's lasted through things, so it's kinda like me. It's nice to have someone cheering me on, even if that "someone" is only a pen.

I grab the notebook and plop onto my bed. My old grey blanket is rough to the touch but comforting nonetheless. I get to work.

Dear Diary,
Wait. I'm not a fifth-grader . . .

March 15
Hi. I'm Bernadette. If I had friends, I would be called Bernie. But I don't. This, apparently, is my new notebook.
My parents died when I was four. We lived in France, and from what I can remember, we really liked it there.

But then my parents died. I only remember one thing from that night. The pounding rain. And the thunder. So much thunder. I try to remember as much as I can, but it's hard, you know? I mean, I was *four*.

Anyway, my uncle enrolled me in a therapy group a few weeks ago. It's terrible. The only thing that makes it somewhat bearable is this girl. Her name is Sam. She seems interesting. Honestly, I just wanna know her deal. She must have something going on, IDK.

I think that's all for now.

March 25
I just got home from therapy. I feel like I tune out everything. Does that happen to everyone? Miss Hunt asked me if I was using my notebook today. I told her no. I'm not gonna give her the satisfaction of thinking she is helping me, even if this notebook thing is actually kinda soothing. Sam wasn't there today. Maybe that's why I zoned out completely. When she's there, I try to get clues as to why she *is* there.

For the rest of April, I wrote in the notebook, and I found it to be the only relief from my crazy world.

I get to therapy early but don't take a seat yet. I walk around the room instead. I actually find some interesting things. There are awards with Miss Hunt's name on them, and there are posters in different fonts and colors. Just then, Sam walks in and takes the seat closest to the door. I slowly creep to the chair next to hers

and sit down, not as gracefully as I could have. She turns her head toward me with a teasing look.

"Nice. As graceful as a ballerina," she says.

I can feel my cheeks burning as I pull my knotted hair around my face. "Yeah."

"Chill out! It was a joke!" She reaches for my shoulder in a comforting manner, but I instinctively swat it away.

"Gosh, chill out. You don't have to be mean about it." She turns away from me, her lavender-scented hair flowing close to my face.

What was that, Bernadette?

I get up and run to the doorway, heading toward the bathroom. When I get there, I run to the closest stall.

Well, that was embarrassing. I need to write that in my notebook.

After a minute of thinking, I decide it's better just to go back and get the notebook than to stay here in the bathroom. I don't care if Sam and I aren't friends. It might be better that way anyway.

I open the stall, go to the sink, and splash water on my face. Then I head back to the room. A few more people came in while I was in the bathroom, but my bag is still on the chair next to Sam, so no one took that seat. As I walk back to where my bag is, I see Sam. In. My. Bag.

"What are you doing?!" I yell at Sam.

She fumbles with something, and throws it into her grey satchel. "Nothing! The bag fell to the ground, so I just picked it up."

I narrow my eyes. "Whatever."

At the end of the session, I pick up my bag and run out the door. I want to get home so I can update my journal.

When I get home, I sprint into my room, almost tripping up the carpeted stairs in the process. My shoes are still on, and I know my uncle won't be happy with me for that, but I don't care.

I enter my room and toss my bag onto my unmade bed. I look inside the bag, but I don't see the notebook. I dump out the contents of the bag and finger through the hairbands and pieces of paper, still not seeing the rainbow hummingbird. Maybe I didn't bring it to therapy? I run to my desk, sifting through all of the binders and pens and pencils. I still don't see it. I empty the contents of my desk drawers. Nothing. I don't really care if I lose it. It can be replaced. But if it isn't here, where is it?

Shoot.

Sam had stuffed something into her bag after I came back from the bathroom. What if she took it?! This is bad. This is really, really bad.

———————

"Bernie!" My uncle yells up to my room. "Time to go to therapy!"

"I don't feel good! Can I stay home today?" I reply. I'm not actually sick, but I can't imagine sitting in the same room as Sam right now.

My uncle comes up to my room and feels my forehead. He's impressed with my "fever" and lets me skip therapy. (Blow-dryer to the forehead works every time.)

I spend the next forty-five minutes

with a piece of paper and a pencil, trying to come up with ways to deal with Sam. All I end up with is this:

- Ignore her for the rest of my life
- Somehow get out of therapy
- Sit across the room every time to avoid confrontation
- Say the notebook wasn't mine (who would it belong to tho??)

I stare at the page for a minute, realizing that none of these things will work.

"Ugh," I say under my breath.

Maybe a good night's rest will give me some ideas.

When did I turn into an old lady thinking everything is fixed with sleep? Whatever.

I put the paper and pencil on my blue nightstand, grab my soft, purple pajamas, and head into my bathroom to shower and change. After a scalding shower, I brush my teeth and fall into bed, getting under the familiar gray fabric. Almost immediately after I close my eyes, I fall asleep.

———————

The next morning, I change into a grey sweatshirt and leggings. I run downstairs to pack my backpack and get breakfast before school. I check the clock on the microwave, and it says 7:30. Great. We're supposed to leave by 7:20 every day to get to school on time. I shove a piece of bread into the toaster. I grab the peanut butter out of the cupboard and my favorite grape jelly out of the fridge. I pull the toast out early because I don't have time to let it fully toast. I smear the peanut butter and jelly onto the bread and grab my backpack from the floor where I had thrown it the day before. The smell of the peanut-butter-and-jelly sandwich makes me smile despite the whole situation with Sam. I hear my uncle honk at me from our silver sedan, so I throw on the first pair of shoes I can find and run out the door.

The next six days are torture, thinking about what to do about Sam and thinking about what was in my notebook that I didn't want anyone else to see.

Eventually, Wednesday rolls around, and despite all my attempts to get out of it, I still end up in that stupid, cold chair. I sit at the chair farthest from the door, hoping that Sam won't notice me when she walks in.

After a few minutes, Sam walks in. She is wearing her navy blue Paddington-style coat and black leggings. She sits a few seats away from me, but it's obvious she saw me. She looks at me, and I look away. After a few moments, I risk a peek at her, and in her hand is my notebook. Before I can look away, Sam gets up and walks over to me. She shyly hands me my notebook.

"This seemed . . . personal."

"Then why did you take it in the first place?" I say.

Sam looks down at her feet. "I don't know."

I sneer at her, look away, and put the notebook back into my bag. When I turn back around, Sam is walking back to her seat, her head drooping.

After therapy that day, I run out of the room as quickly as possible, trying to avoid confrontation.

The next few days of school were pretty terrible, but finally it was the weekend. I get out my geography homework and start labeling the map when my uncle walks in.

"Hey," he says.

"Hey," I reply, still doing my work at my desk.

"There is someone here for you." He says.

I spin around, and there, in my doorway, is Sam.

"What are you doing here?" I say, a little too loudly. My uncle gives me a look. I roll my eyes, and he leaves the room.

"What are you doing here?" I ask again, a little quieter than before.

"I wanted to apologize for stealing your notebook. I didn't have any right to take it."

"That's right. You didn't have any right to take it." I turn away and face my homework.

I can tell Sam sits on the bed because of the squeaking sound my bed makes.

"Look. That isn't the only reason I came here. I wanted to tell you 'my deal.'" Sam says quietly.

I turn to face her, partly irritated but partly intrigued.

Sam takes a steadying breath, and she begins to speak. "My parents divorced two years ago. My family was torn apart. I mean, I have three siblings! My mom started dating a guy two months after she got divorced, and it seemed like she had just tossed my dad off like a piece of trash. Then, three months after that, my mother got married to that guy. Nine months later, my other little sister, Posie, was born. My dad got really depressed after the divorce and started drinking again. One night, he was driving drunk and got into a car crash. He's still alive, but he hit his head really badly, and he can't do almost anything without someone's help."

"Oh my gosh. I'm so sorry" is all I could come up with.

Sam looks down.

"I guess one reason I wanted to read your notebook was to see that I wasn't alone, you know? Everyone is always telling me that there are people struggling like me out there, but I have never met anyone like that. And I'm pretty sure that therapy isn't going to help."

"Well, think about this. If you didn't want to tell me your deal, do you think that someone who is struggling like you will just come right out and say it?" I ask her.

Sam looks down. "No, I guess not."

"Right." I give her a smile.

Sam cracks a small smile. "Thank you, Bernie."

Reflections
(iPhone 8 Plus)
Analise Braddock, 9
Katonah, NY

Highlights from StoneSoup.com

From the Stone Soup Blog

Loneliness
By Salma Hadi-St. John, 11
Oak Park, IL

My friends are all gone
My life has disappeared
Into a new world of loneliness
It is just my family and I

Loneliness is like a tree in the desert
The only cat in town
A star stuck in space
A speck of dust in the air

Loneliness is when you are the only one
At your birthday party
When you sit on the steps of your porch
On a dark rainy day

It feels like I am trapped inside
Waiting for people to come
Watching the clock on the wall
Scratching the door like a dog

But sometimes you just have to fight
Loneliness
You can't be alone everyday

When I wake up today
It is the start of a new day

We can be a force together
We just need to reach out for each other
Feeling happiness again

About the Stone Soup Blog

We publish original work—writing, art, book reviews, and multimedia projects—by young people on the Stone Soup Blog. When the pandemic began, we got so much incredible writing about the experience of living through the lockdowns that we created a special category for it! You can read more posts by young bloggers, and find out more about submitting a blog post, here: https://stonesoup.com/stone-soup-blog/.

Honor Roll

Welcome to the Stone Soup Honor Roll. Every month, we receive submissions from hundreds of kids from around the world. Unfortunately, we don't have space to publish all the great work we receive. We want to commend some of these talented writers and artists and encourage them to keep creating.

STORIES

Lyla Carr, 12
Helen LaForge, 12
Jasper Martin, 11
Suman Shah, 10

POETRY

Arnit Dey, 12
Tiffany Oller, 7
Madeline Roy, 9
Evelyn Worcester, 13

ART

Maggie Kershen, 11
Keshavan Rao, 7

CPSIA information can be obtained
at www.ICGtesting.com
Printed in the USA
JSHW020152020221
11446JS00001B/10